Breaking the Rules

Maxine Linnell

A & C Black • London

To Kate

First published 2012 by A & C Black,
an imprint of Bloomsbury Publishing Plc
50 Bedford Square, London WC1B 3DP

www.acblack.com

Copyright © 2012 Maxine Linnell
Illustrations copyright © 2012 Sophie Escabasse

The rights of Maxine Linnell and Sophie Escabasse to be identified
as the author and illustrator of this work have been asserted by them
in accordance with the Copyrights, Designs and Patents Act 1988.

ISBN 978-1-4081-5271-3

A CIP catalogue for this book is available from the British Library.

This book is produced using paper that is made from wood
grown in managed, sustainable forests. It is natural, renewable
and recyclable. The logging and manufacturing processes conform
to the environmental regulations of the country of origin.

Printed by CPI Group (UK), Croydon, CR0 4YY

recommended by

www.catchup.org

Catch Up is a not-for-profit charity
which aims to address the problem of
underachievement that has its roots in
literacy and numeracy difficulties.

Contents

Chapter One

Making Friends

Monday.

This morning will be different. This week will be different. I'll make it different. I'm going to make an effort.

I found this website – *makingfriends.com*. They tell you how to do it. To make friends.

So I've got these rules now, for making friends with people.

I don't understand people. Sometimes I don't even think I like people. I bet it won't work.

But the website says you have to think positive. So I'm telling myself it will work. It's got to.

I'm going to talk to somebody at school. Anybody. I will smile. I will even go up to the class loser and ask her how she is. I will speak to somebody today. I will hold my head up and look them in the eye.

My first rule is *Make an effort*. I'll do it. I can, I know I can.

I realise I'm smiling. That's a first since I got to this dump. I mean, this lovely new place. I must remember to think positive.

I get to school early. Dad makes me walk, but I can do that. I can do anything. School is miles away. Well, it takes about twenty minutes. It feels like miles.

I stop off at the gate, watching for anyone I half know.

"Hi," I say, smiling, when four girls from my class swoop by. "How're you doing?"

They're chatting too much and laughing too loudly to hear me. They don't stop. I'm left on my own. Again. But I won't get down about it.

I trail after them into the classroom.

Make an effort, I say to myself.

"Hi," I say, grinning at the class loser, landing my bag on the table next to hers.

Her mouth drops open in shock. "Hi," she mutters.

Then she turns away and looks down at the book she's got open on the table. She'd rather look at a stupid book than talk to me. Now who's the loser?

I think I'll give up now. This is not working.

Chapter Two

New Life, No Life

Mo. That's my name. Not that anyone cares.

I've been at this school for a whole week. We've moved to a new town halfway across the country. It's nothing like where I used to live in Bristol. It's not like home.

Mum says this is home now and I have to stop comparing it to Bristol.

This is more like hell. Whatever hell is. I'm not sure I believe in hell. But this place is rock solid real.

I wish it was made up.

One day someone will come up to me and say, "Hey, I've been wanting to talk to you ever since you got here. You're just so interesting. The way you look – not like any of the others. You've got style. Want to come out on Friday?"

It won't happen. I'll just wander round the playing field at lunch time like I'm looking for something, or someone.

I *am* looking for something. My life.

Because I used to have a life, and now I've lost it.

I'm Mo. I've got frizzy hair, Tesco jeans, no special talents except whining.

My dad lost his job in Bristol. I mean, he didn't even like his job. He was always moaning on about it. Stupid job. Stupid boss. Not enough money. Too many hours. Not enough holidays.

So what did he do when he lost it? He got a new job and made everyone move to a new town.

How selfish is that? Did he ask me? Did he think about anyone but himself?

And he doesn't even like the new job.

It's just the same as before. Stupid job, stupid boss, not enough money, too many hours, not enough holidays.

My mum tells me we had to move. Now she has to work in a supermarket. She's looking older. And she's lost all her friends too, just like me. And Gran is back in Bristol, phoning every day, forgetting where we are, wanting Mum to come round or do the shopping.

Mum cries or shouts at me and Jack every time Gran phones.

I tell her, "It's not my fault we're here, you should have told Dad you weren't going," and then Mum cries some more.

"It's not like that," she says. "It's not like that."

I don't know what to say.

Jack's my little brother. He's eleven, with sandy hair and freckles, full of jokes and chat.

Everyone likes Jack. He's okay at school. He was straight into the football team, racing round the pitch, people trying to catch his eye, calling his name. They know his name. It took him five minutes to settle in, even though it's the middle of autumn term.

In my class I get to sit by the loser. She doesn't seem to care what she looks like. She just works. She reads loads. And from what I can tell she's always getting the best marks.

Even she doesn't talk to me.

I don't know any of these people. My friends back home were the best. Alex and Jemma. We had such good times. I wish they were here. I wish I was there with them.

I must think positive. Make an effort. Those are the rules.

They had all these stories, on the website, about people who went from no friends at all to millions of friends, just by following the rules. Did they make the stories up?

I have to think positive. I have to try harder.

Chapter Three

Facebooking

It's night. It's dark. It's cold. I'm on Facebook. Jemma is online and we're chatting. She used to live near me. We used to spend all our time together, with Alex of course, and some of the others. Now she lives a million miles away.

Jemma
How are you doing?

I bet it's obvious how I'm doing if you can see me. But she's too far away to see.

Mo
Cool. It's great here, loads of new friends and everything. Can't believe it's only a week since I got here

Why can't I tell the truth? But I don't want to tell her the truth. What's the point?

Jemma
We're all going out on Friday, sleepover at Alex's. Her birthday, remember?

Do I remember? Alex, my best friend.
Forever. Before I got sent away. Before Dad
dragged me to this dump.

Mo
Yeah. I'm going out too. With some
mates.

I wish.

Jemma
Where are you going?

Mo
I dunno, movie or something.

Jemma
Cool.

And she's gone.

I look through everyone's news.
Break-ups, make-ups, who's single, who's in
a relationship, photos of parties I'm not at.
Everyone's having a great time in Bristol.

Since when did I tell lies and make things
up?

Since I came here.

I can't let it get to me. I have to make an
effort. That's the rule. Rule number one.

Rule number two is: *I have to think
positive.*

I play games for a while, check my email.
Then go back to Facebook.

There's a new guy asking to be a friend.

At least *some*one wants to be my friend. I wonder who he is. Should I say yes?

Look. He wants to be my friend. Right? Am I going to reject the one person who's interested in me? Kind of?

I click on confirm and don't think about it again.

I'll do the school gate routine again tomorrow. That's another rule. *I have to try three times*. So that means two more days.

I just made up that rule. But hey, I can change the rules.

Chapter Four

Total Idiot

It's Tuesday. I didn't sleep much at all.
And when I did sleep, I had horrible dreams.
People ignoring me. Me running after them,
calling out, shouting, but never catching them.
Just like real life.

I do the school gate routine again. A girl in my class looks at me, then smiles. I don't think she meant to.

A boy gives me a look and sniggers to his friend. As if I'd be interested in him.

I go and sit by the loser again. She's reading and making notes in a book. She doesn't even look up.

In the playing fields at lunch-time, I wander about. It's windy and I pull my sweatshirt sleeves down over my hands to keep them warm.

The same girl, the one who smiled, comes over and talks to me. She's taller than me, Asian, big eyes, long straight black hair. I wish I had hair like that.

She's talking to me, smiling. I'm so shocked I don't hear what she says.

But I get the last bit.

"Come over, we're just having a laugh."

I mumble something about meeting a friend. She shrugs and walks away.

Why did I do that? How could I be so stupid? I'm such a total idiot.

Chapter Five

Shopping Hell

School's finished for the day. I don't want to go home. The evening stretches out, empty. I don't want to just sit in my room again.

I turn towards town, or what they call town here. I haven't had a look at the shops.

There was too much to do last weekend sorting out my bedroom after the move.

So this is it.

Call it a town? Call these shops? There is nowhere – like, *nowhere*, none of these shops – that I'd buy anything from. I want to turn round and go home. But I must make an effort. I might have missed something.

I wander round. No, there's nothing. And everyone else my age is with their mates. In a two, or a three, or a four. Having fun. The only people on their own are in a hurry. They have places to go and people to see. Homes that they want to go to.

I'm staring at a charity shop window.

There's china dogs, a set of cups and saucers, and a dress on a stand that looks like it's there to get people in, but it puts me right off.

I could offer to give them some advice on how to run a shop so people like me would go in. I could transform the whole place, make it somewhere anyone would want to be, make the charity millions. Then do a TV programme about how I did it.

I look at the sign. It's a charity for old people. They don't want people like me in there. That's why they've got a dress my nan would turn down.

I go on down the street. I see one of those cheap clothes shops and go inside.

Maybe if I had clothes from here people would talk to me? I mean, this is where they must buy stuff, right? There's no other clothes shops.

There's not much, but I pick out some jeans and a top and go to try them on.

I'm finding my way into the jeans in the changing cubicle, when I hear a familiar voice.

"What do you think? I mean, they're not too bad, are they? Do they fit my bum?" the voice says.

I pull up the jeans and zip them. They are truly terrible.

They're all laughing out there.

"No, they're fine – you look good in them," someone says.

"You should get them – wear them on Saturday," adds another voice.

I pull back the curtain and step out into the corridor. By the mirror, posing with her mates, is the girl who spoke to me this morning. And she's got the same jeans on as me.

I am so embarrassed.

She sees, of course. They all see. There's even the same label on the front, saying 'reduced'. The worst thing is, they suit her much better than me.

"Hi," the girl says, "you buying those?"

"No, they're so – I mean – maybe," I mumble.

She knows what I'm saying. What I'm thinking.

"No, me neither."

The others go quiet.

I back into the changing cubicle again. I don't even try the top. I wait until I can't hear them any more.

I can't help it, my eyes are welling up and I can't stop crying. I'm glad they're playing crap music so nobody will hear.

When they've all gone I come out of the cubicle and dump the clothes with the girl.

Chapter Six

Shadow

The bloke I friended on Facebook has written on my wall. His name's Shadow. What kind of name is that?

 Shadow
Did you used to be in Bristol? I'm sure I remember your face from somewhere.

I send him a message. I don't want
everyone to know my business.

Mo
Yeah, until I moved to this dump.
Brinckley, whoever's even heard of
Brinckley?

He answers right away, like he's waiting.

Shadow
Hey. That's strange. I moved away
too. I'm in Derby. It's not so bad
here, not far from Brinckley as it
happens.

I'm chatting to him for about an hour. I
feel better. He's interesting. 19, at college,
on some kind of scheme where they work
part-time. Lives with his mates. Goes out to
clubs. He's funny. He asks me questions.

He listens.

I don't need to try. Or lie. Or think positive.

I'm going to do the gate thing one more time. It's the rule. But tomorrow I'm going to try something else as well. Another rule. *Listen to people*. On the website it says, if you want people to listen to you, you have to listen to them.

Why shouldn't they listen to me first? I mean, I could tell them all about the cool places in Bristol, and my really great friends, and the amazing shops. Or maybe that wouldn't work. Maybe better not.

Listen, and try everything three times. Those are the rules.

Or maybe twice.

Chapter Seven

Bad Art

Wednesday.

It's freezing. It's the last day of my gate routine. The girl who smiled yesterday comes past.

I say "hi", not expecting anything.

And she stops.

"What're you doing hanging round here?" she says. "It's so cold, you'll freeze."

"Yeah." I can't tell her about the rules.

I look at my hands. I think they're turning blue. And my feet, they're icy too. I'm not sure anyone would notice if I got frostbite and my feet fell off. Or maybe even if I died. Would anyone come to the funeral? Would they look really guilty and sad, because they should have listened and everything?

I realise I'm not listening to this girl, and she's standing looking at me.

"You doing anything at break?" she says.

Her name's Mahsuda. If I've spelled that right. I heard one of her mates calling her that.

I want to say yes. I take a deep breath, and nothing comes out.

"We're going to the art room," she says. "It's warm in there. Miss Stanton doesn't mind. Want to come?"

I don't really fancy it. I'm not an arty person. But I grit my teeth. Remember the rules. "Okay," I say.

"See you later then," she says. She moves on, runs to catch up with her friends.

Result. Maybe. Maybe the teacher told her to make friends with the new saddo.

Last Monday, when I first got to school, he made a speech. "This is Mo. She's new here – to Brinckley and to this school. Now, it's not easy being new in mid-term.

So I want everyone to look out for her, show her round."

Everyone turned round and looked at me. Then they turned back and went on talking to their friends.

But she's invited me now, and I said yes. Think positive. It is a result.

I can't wait for break. I can't focus on anything. Nobody notices, of course. But that's a good thing right now.

I go to the art room, and there's a huddle of four girls and a few boys scattered about. Mahsuda's in the middle of the huddle.

I hover round, pretending to look at the art. I hope she notices me soon.

The art is bad. You'd think it was done by four-year-olds, not people doing their GCSEs. I could do this. And I'm no good at art.

Then Mahsuda sees me.

"You came! Hey, have you seen what Joe's done?" she asks.

I don't know anyone called Joe, except in Bristol. He was this tall guy with a beard who walked in the park looking suspect.

Mahsuda is waiting, looking at me. I think I've forgotten how to have a conversation.

"Who's Joe?" I ask. That's good, that's listening, isn't it?

She laughs like a drain.

"Hey, Mo doesn't know who Joe is!

How can anyone not know who Joe is? Joe," she says, turning her back on me and swinging her hips to the others, "is the coolest boy in Brinckley."

I'm not impressed. Can she tell? No, not with her back to me she can't. But I have to keep this going.

"Wow," I say, "and you know him?"

Another question, that's good. Do I sound like I mean it?

"Do I know him?" she says. Everyone laughs.

"Course she knows him, he lives on her street," says one of the others.

"That," says Mahsuda, "is Luce, and that," pointing her finger, "is Taz, and this is Suki."

Luce looks the other way. She's blonde, long hair, about my height. Taz is dark-skinned, tall, ought to be a model. Suki's little, kind of chunky, looks the most friendly of them. She smiles at me.

I smile back. She keeps smiling. This is embarrassing.

I have to keep it going. "So what's Joe done?"

"Only cartoons of all the teachers – look, they're on that wall. And he doesn't flatter any of them," says Luce.

I don't know who the teachers are, but I pretend to be interested. And I recognise the teacher who gave the speech about me. I'm glad Joe made him look stupid.

Say something. Make it a question. "So what do you guys do round here?"

Better. Mahsuda takes the lead again.

"I," she says, "watch Joe. And Luce watches me. And Taz – Taz is just Taz. And Suki studies – don't you, Suki? When she's not looking after everyone. She's going to be a doctor, aren't you, Suki? And what – Mo – do you do round here?"

I can't believe these people. Do they always talk like people in a reality show?

Mahsuda looks at me and laughs. "Sorry, you look so awkward. I couldn't resist it."

"You're cruel, M," says Luce, laughing.

"We're not that bad, honest," says Taz.

They all laugh. Even Taz.

They're laughing at me.

I want to be sick. I thought I was doing so well. I can't wait for the end of the day, and I get out as soon as I can.

Back home, there's a message from Shadow. I decide to play cool, keep him guessing. Don't answer for at least twenty minutes. I might make that a rule. Well, ten minutes. Then we start chatting.

And then it's nine o'clock and Mum's shouting at me about homework and all that. I suppose I'd better get on with it.

But he's cool, Shadow. He's funny, like I said. He's not like the others.

Chapter Eight

Dad's Fault

Thursday morning.

It's cold, it's wet. Outside it's pouring down. It never rained like this in Bristol.

I get up too late for breakfast and Mum and Dad shout at me.

"In that car before I count to ten or you're walking," yells Dad. He's been so stressed since we got here, it's unbelievable.

But I know he means what he says.

I'm in the passenger seat in seconds. No way am I going to walk in this weather. But I haven't brushed my teeth, and I haven't got my homework.

"I haven't got my homework," I say.

"Tough," he says. "You want a lift, you get up in time. I have to be at work. No use losing this job, after everything."

"I'll get into trouble," I tell him.

"Tough," he says again, settling into the driver's seat and blasting me with cold air.

"I'll tell them it's your fault," I say.

Dad whistles, in a really irritating way. I don't know why he does that, he knows it winds everyone up. Specially me.

I say it louder. "I'll tell them, it's because you're a bad father and you don't give me time to get ready for school."

He drives off, just missing a bus that pulls out. He blares the horn, as if it wasn't his fault. It's embarrassing. At school he drums his fingers on the steering wheel until I climb out and slam the door. Then he goes off without even saying goodbye.

It's not a good start. And I'm late. That's his fault too.

I don't wait at the gate. Why would I, in this rain? I'm not stupid.

Anyway, I did it three times and it didn't work. So that rule's gone.

I've got the new one now. Listening. If only Dad listened. Or Mum. Anybody.

Mahsuda's at the door, watching out.

"Hi Mahsuda, how're you doing?"

"Hi Mo. Fine thanks. Seen Luce or Suki?"

"No, perhaps they're late. Had a good night last night?" I ask. Two sentences, that's good.

"Just telly and homework. You?" asks Mo.

"Chatting to this guy I met on Facebook. He's cool," I say.

Her eyebrows go up. "You know him?" she asks.

"Well, no, not exactly. But he comes from Bristol too, and he's in Derby."

I'm going to tell her more, but Suki arrives with Luce, and the teacher too. He looks pleased to see me talking to them. He probably thinks it's down to his little talk. It's just as I thought.

I get into trouble about the homework. I tell them it's Dad's fault. But they don't listen. Nobody listens.

I hate this place.

It's half past eight at night. I've shouted at Dad, and Mum. I've told them I hate them.

I wouldn't eat the pasta dish Mum got from the place where she works. It was past its sell-by date. She said it would be fine, and I said she was trying to poison me.

She said there wasn't anything else.

Jack ran off to his bedroom holding his ears. Then Mum sent me upstairs too. I'm hungry.

Shadow's online. I tell him about it. The way Dad rushed me to school and made me forget my homework. The way people get at me. The way everyone makes out it's my fault.

Mo
But it's not my fault!

Shadow
No babe, it's not your fault. Sounds like you need some time out.

Shadow
How about coming to Derby on Saturday afternoon? We could go round the shops, have a coffee?

I wait for a bit. I'm not sure. I don't really know him.

Mo
Where would we meet?

Shadow
How about coming in on the train and I'll meet you at the station?

Mo
I'm not sure.

Shadow
Go on, take a risk. You might enjoy it.

Take a risk. Maybe that's what I should do. I've tried being nice and listening to people and none of it works. I should take a risk.

Try three times. That's the rule.

I don't need a dumb website to tell me how to live. I'll make up my own rules.

Mo
Okay.

Chapter Nine

Thank God It's...

Friday.

I walk into school. My bag's heavy, but it's better this way than going with Dad. I turn a corner and bump into Suki. It turns out she lives on the next road to mine.

We're chatting. Really chatting.

"What're you doing tomorrow?" she asks.

"I'm – I'm meeting this guy – in Derby."

"Who is he?" she asks.

"His name's Shadow. I met him on Facebook. He used to live in Bristol like me. He's really kind and thoughtful. He's listened to me going on about how bad my life is, and he's – he's just there, you know?"

"Do your parents know you're meeting him?" asks Suki

"No way, I'm not telling them," I say. "They'd find a way of spoiling it. They do that with everything."

"Is it really bad, your life?" she asks me.

I feel awkward, opening up to her like this. I mean, I don't know her or anything. She could just blab it all to everyone and they'll laugh at me even more.

But today I'm taking risks. It's my own rule. So I tell her. She listens. We're at school before I've finished, and we're swept up in everything.

I feel a bit better though.

Till break, when I go to the art room, and nobody's there. I imagine them all laughing while Suki tells them every word I've said. I think of Luce and Taz sniggering. Mahsuda making some kind of sarcastic comment. And them never speaking to me again.

Suki comes up to me at lunch time.

"When you meeting this guy then?" she says.

"Tomorrow. I'll get the 1.15 train."

She looks a bit strange, then Luce comes up and they go off together.

They don't invite me to go with them. I feel so stupid. I can't wait to see Shadow tomorrow.

I walk round the playing fields for a while, then I go in the library. Just for somewhere to go. I get through the afternoon, and the evening.

Shadow isn't on Facebook tonight. I wonder if he'll turn up. I wonder what he's like. I wonder if I should go. But it's the rule. Take a risk. What else is there to do?

Chapter Ten

The Meeting

Saturday. Two whole days off school.

Dad is doing DIY in the shed. Or that's
what he says he's doing. He never did DIY
before. We never had a shed before. But it's
not a big shed.

Mum is in serious mother mode. She's in the kitchen. It's tiny. This whole house is like a doll's house. It's new, on three floors. You're always going up and downstairs. All the rooms are too small.

Dad says it's just till we find our feet. I know where my feet are. I don't know where he thinks his are. I imagine his feet going off without him. Maybe he's making new ones in the shed.

"What are your plans for today?" Mum asks me. "I've got the day off work, I thought we could go shopping or something. Check out Derby."

I can't go to Derby with my mum! I can't!

"No, I can't," I say.

"But I've got today off, and you've looked so down since you've been here," she says. "I thought I'd give you a treat. We could find somewhere for lunch, look at the clothes."

"I'm meeting some of the girls from school later," I say. "We might go over to Derby on the train, I don't know."

It's a lie, of course. Another one.

"Oh, that's good news," says Mum, trying to look happy for me. "You're making friends then?"

"Yeah – there's Mahsuda, and Luce, and Suki. And Taz. We're all meeting up."

Call them friends? I don't trust any of them. How do I know what they're saying behind my back?

"Oh." She looks disappointed. "Well, your dad's in the shed, doing who knows what. Jack's out playing football. I suppose I'll do the housework."

I want, so much, to give her a hug and say I'll go to Derby with her, we'll have a good time, like we did in Bristol. I almost do. But I've got a risk to take.

I check out the internet. Shadow's online.

Shadow
You coming then?

Mo
Yeah, sure. How will I know you?

Shadow
I'll find you. I've seen your photo.
On the forecourt, 1.45.

I get ready. I don't want to look too keen,
so I just put on some make-up, do my hair
and put jeans and a sweatshirt on. It's a good
look. Not too keen. Keen enough.

I will do it, I will. But I'm scared.

Think positive.

Mum's in the kitchen, loading up the
washing machine. I don't know if I want kids
when I'm grown up. Too much hard work.

"Bye," I say to her back.

"Bye," she mumbles to the washing.
"What time will you be home?"

I shrug my shoulders. "Dunno," I say, leaving before she can argue.

She's not happy, that's clear. But I've got to get a life, somehow.

I walk down to the station. It's one o'clock when I get there, and I buy my ticket and sit on a bench. There's loads of people waiting. Looks like there's a football match on.

The train comes and I have to stand all the way. I'm glad I didn't put my heels on. I'd be in total agony. But what if he wants to take me to a posh restaurant? What if he's really cool, and he's dressed up?

It's only one stop, so I can't get off. The time goes by really quick. I want it to last longer.

There's a fit guy standing next to me, but he's talking football to his friend all the way. I think I've gone invisible while I wasn't looking.

I get off the train in Derby and head for the ticket barrier. It is so crowded. There's no way anyone will find me here.

And the fans are all singing. The police are there too. It doesn't feel safe.

I hope Shadow turns up and rescues me soon.

I look in Smiths, buy a bottle of water and take a swig. My heart is racing. I don't look at anyone. It is so odd not knowing what he looks like. Why didn't I think of that before?

The noise begins to fade. It's almost two o'clock. The people go – to the match, I suppose.

Now there's nobody in the shop but me. I begin to feel embarrassed, waiting there.

I go out of the shop and look at the coffees in the drinks stall. I've got my back to everything. I wish I'd never come.

I'm sure he won't turn up. Why should he, anyway? I'm just some sad girl he met on Facebook. I bet he's going to the match with his mates. Bet he's laughing about it with them. Bet he's seeing somebody else.

I turn round, just to have a look. Quickly.

There's someone by the leaflets. A bloke.

He must be about thirty, at least. He's got saggy jeans on, and a grey tee shirt. He doesn't look good.

That can't be him. It can't be.

He's reading a leaflet. It's obvious he's just waiting. He looks at his watch.

I don't know what to do.

He turns towards me. He's walking up to me.

I don't know what to do.

Now it's too risky. He's not who I thought he was – he's not who he said he was. He lied to me. Like I lied. But not to him. I never lied to him. I told him everything that was happening. And he listened. But he's old enough to be my dad!

I wish my dad was here.

The guy's coming closer. It must be him. "Mo – is it Mo?" he says.

I don't know what to say. He's a stranger. He isn't who I thought, or what I wanted.

I just wanted a friend. Someone to meet up with. Someone to talk to.

And I was following the rules. Taking a risk.

But not this risk. Not this man.

I can't breathe. I can't move. He's still there. He's come up close. I can see his skin, greasy, and his hair's not clean. Why did I take so much trouble?

"It's Mo?" he says again.

"Yes, I mean, no," I say.

He smiles. "Which is it?"

I can't speak.

He takes my arm. "Let's get out of here, shall we?"

I can't move. I don't want to move. I want to get out of here, but not with him.

Then I see her. Mahsuda. She's peering round the wall from the car park.

Then there's Luce, on the other side. And Suki, coming from the ticket office. And Taz, wandering over.

Shadow's looking round. He drops my arm.

"Hi, Mo, really good to see you." It's Mahsuda, taking the lead as usual.

I am so glad to see her.

"Who's this creep?" says Luce, edging in front of Shadow.

"Hey – " starts Shadow, but he doesn't have a chance.

The girls link arms with me and we walk through the arch into the car park. I get some words out at last.

"What are you doing here?"

"Let's get out of here first, then we'll tell," says Luce.

We walk out into the sunshine. I can breathe again. They're laughing, and I join in.

"How did you know – how did you get here?" I ask.

"You told us – you didn't tell any of us all of it, but we put everything together…" Mahsuda begins.

"…and we thought, this doesn't sound good," adds Suki.

I feel a bit offended that they were talking about me, but I'm so glad to get out that I don't mind. At least they were listening.

"We thought we'd come over on the earlier train – then we could make sure we could see you without giving it all away," Mahsuda goes on.

"We can't let a friend down, can we? We couldn't let you get into trouble," says Luce.

A friend. She called me a friend.

"I'd have been alright," I begin, then stop. "No, I'm glad you came. I mean – taking risks is one thing, but that was going too far."

"Taking risks?" Suki asks.

I tell them about the rules. They listen. They don't laugh. They seem to understand.

"I was new, when I came here from Birmingham," says Luce. "I hated it. And these guys didn't make it any easier – until they came round. They do in the end."

"It's just our way," says Mahsuda. "It's embarrassing, living in Brinckley. I can't wait to get out. And Bristol – it sounds fantastic – was it good to live there?"

And they listen to my stories about Bristol, and we go shopping, and we have a coffee and by the time we get on the train back everything looks different, everything's changed.

And I've dumped the rules. For now, anyway.

Chapter Eleven

New Start

Sunday.

We had a great day yesterday, me and the others. We went to a movie in the evening, and it was fun. I haven't forgotten how to talk to people after all.

The rules – I suppose they were okay. Only I chose the wrong person to trust, to listen to.

If I'd gone with him, I don't know what would have happened. I've heard all those stories, would it have been like that? Drugs, prostitution, all of it?

Or was he just a lonely sad bloke looking for a friend? That makes me feel a bit bad about getting away from him.

But he told me lies. Everything he said about himself, about college, his age, all lies, every bit of it. Why would anyone do that?

Then I remember my lies, to Jemma, to Mum.

I go down to the kitchen. Mum's reading the paper.

"D'you want to go shopping today?" I ask. "I went to Derby yesterday, I know all the good shops. I'll show you around. And there's loads of places to eat, for lunch."

A frown crosses her face, then she puts the paper down.

"Yeah – Dad can do something with Jack, and you and me, we'll have some serious girl time, shall we?"

I go over and give her a hug. "D'you know, Mum?" I say.

"What?" she asks.

"I think it might be okay here after all."